There Was a Speech Teacher Who Swallowed Some Dice

by Patricia L. Mervine, M.A., CCC-SLP
Illustrated by Ian Acker

About the Author: Patricia L. Mervine is a speech/language pathologist, assistive technology consultant, and children's book author. She has been working for over 20 years to improve the communication skills of children who have a variety of disabilities.

Pat is the creator of the popular web site, www.speakingofspeech.com, and the blog, www.speakingofspeech.blog.com, two valuable resources for SLPs, teachers, parents, and others who support children who have communication impairments.

You can learn more about Pat and her books at her author site, www.patmervine.com.

Other books by Pat Mervine, available through www.patmervine.com:

How Katie Got a Voice (and a cool new nickname)

Wie Katie eine Stimme bekam (und einen coolen Spitznamen) -German edition

The Mouth With a Mind of Its Own

ISBN-13: 978-1500214944

ISBN-10: 1500214949

"So, Johnny, what did you do in speech today?"

"We played a game."

There was a Speech Teacher
who swallowed some dice.
They rattled and rolled,
but didn't feel nice.

Did they land on a six,

a five, or a three?

She swallowed a mirror,

hoping to see.

But inside her insides
it was dark as midnight.

"Aha!" she thought.

"I need a flashlight."

So down went the light,
quick as you please.
Still hungry, she swallowed
some old IEPs.

Sadly, as always,

these made her uneasy.

And chewing on data forms

made her quite queasy.

She ate up some games

for stuttering and listening.

Then, off in the distance,

she
        saw
                something
                        glistening.

What was it? Oh, my!

Sound cards by the deck!

"Should I eat them?"

she wondered,

then thought,

"What the heck!"

She gobbled them down with
a tongue depressor or two,
a timer, three posters,
some scissors and glue.

There Was a Speech Teacher Who Swallowed Some Dice

by Patricia L. Mervine, M.A., CCC-SLP
Illustrated by Ian Acker

"What's next?," you wonder.

Guess what she took!

That silly Speech Teacher

ate a silly kids' book!

She swallowed a prize box
and an "I ♥ Speech" sticker.
Then she felt sick....

.....then sicker....

......and sicker.

Her plan book and schedule
tasted quite sour.
The poor Speech Teacher
felt worse by the hour.

Suddenly, those dice....
they shook and they rolled.
And what happened next
was amazing, I'm told.

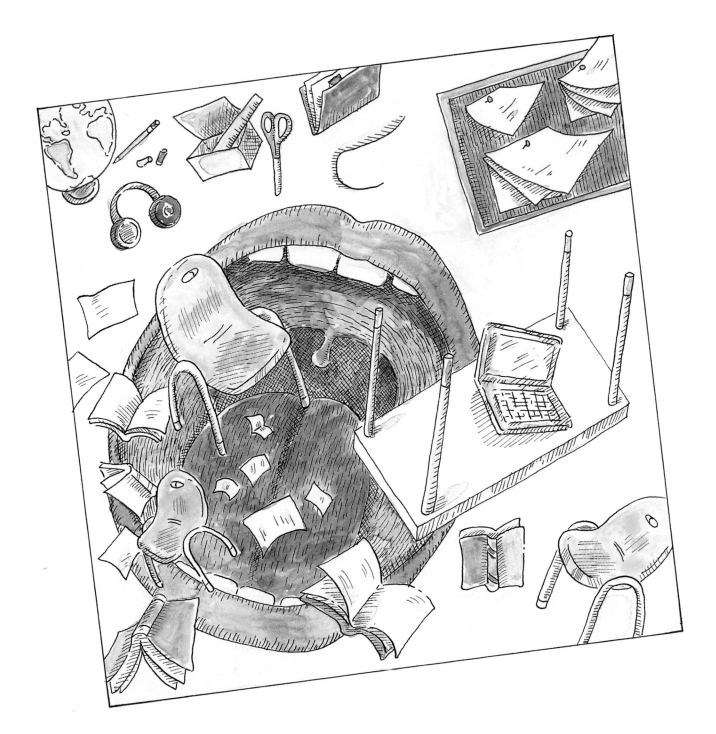

That poor Speech Teacher, feeling misery and doom, burped up a speech/language therapy room!

A place where kids talk,

a place where kids play,

improving their speech

and their language all day.

Are you new to Speech?

Don't even think twice!

You will learn, too!

Just don't swallow the dice.

What do Speech-Language Pathologists (SLPs) use in therapy?

Although the title "Speech Teacher" is used in this story, the professional title is "Speech-Language Pathologist."

In this story, the Speech Teacher swallows lots of things that you will find in most speech/language therapy rooms. Here is a list of the items she swallows and why they are in her room:

- **Dice and board games:** Improving your speech and language can be hard work, so SLPs make it fun and keep students interested by playing games once in a while.

- **Mirror and flashlight:** When working on speech sounds like /r/, which can be very hard to see, it is very helpful for a student to look inside his or her mouth with a flashlight to see what the tongue is doing and where it is supposed to be to make better speech sounds.

- **IEPs:** This stands for Individualized Education Program. Nearly all students who work with an SLP have an IEP. This is a legal document that lists the student's goals and describes ways in which the student will be helped to achieve those goals. The IEP is reviewed at least once each year by the student's parents, teacher, school administrator, SLP, and anyone else who is working with the student on IEP goals.

- **Data forms:** SLPs take a lot of data! That means that the SLP takes notes during therapy sessions and often counts how many times the student does something correctly or incorrectly. Data can be collected on a scratch pad, sticky notes, checklists and other forms, and even on a tablet or smart phone. Sometimes, students take their own data. This information helps the SLP plan therapy lessons that target specific IEP goals.

- **Sound cards:** Nearly every SLP has a supply of cards with words and pictures on them, organized by the speech sounds that the students are working to improve. Clever SLPs can think of hundreds of ways to use these cards!

- **Prize box and stickers:** Not all SLPs give prizes and stickers, but many who work with young children do. Students usually have to earn these treats by following the SLP's rules and working hard in therapy.

- **Tongue depressors**: These, and other tools made to go into the mouth, can help students get their tongues in the correct position for better speech sounds.

- **Timer:** SLPs can use a timer to set a specific time for short periods of practice within a therapy session, and to measure how long or how often specific speech or other behaviors occur within a set time period.

- **Scissors and glue:** SLPs often use craft projects to teach children basic concepts, how to listen and follow directions, and other therapy goals.

- **Posters:** SLPs often decorate their rooms with posters that teach, motivate, and make the room a nice place to be.

- **Books:** SLPs use all kinds of books in therapy — picture books, chapter books, even text books — to work on many skills, including articulation, vocabulary, reading, and writing.

- **Plan book:** SLPs keep a record of what happens during each therapy session. Some SLPs write their notes in a plan book. Others type their notes on a computer or tablet. The plan book can also contain lesson plans for future therapy sessions.

- **Schedule:** SLPs always follow a schedule of therapy sessions, and that schedule is usually very busy!

Therapy Room Scavenger Hunt

Check off each item you find in the therapy room, then use your best speech and language to describe each item's location and use.

_____ Dice	_____ Board Games
_____ Mirror	_____ Flashlight
_____ Sound Cards	_____ Prize Box
_____ Stickers	_____ Tongue Depressors
_____ Timer	_____ Scissors
_____ Glue	_____ Plan Book
_____ Data Forms	_____ IEPs
_____ Schedule	_____ Posters

What are your goals in speech/language therapy? _____

_____

Find your name on your SLP's schedule. When do you come to therapy?

_____

Made in the USA
San Bernardino, CA
27 August 2016